BLUE BURT
and
WIGGLES

Written and illustrated by
Derek Anderson

Simon & Schuster Books for Young Readers

New York   London   Toronto   Sydney

Blue Burt and Wiggles were the best of friends.
They played together all summer long.

But summer was going away. The leaves were falling, the grass was turning brown, and all the birds in the north woods were heading south.

Blue Burt would have to leave soon too.

"Hey, Blue Burt," squawked Mo the Crow. "You'd better come now or you'll freeze your feathers."
Mo was right. So Blue Burt went to pack up.

Blue Burt was sorting through his things when he discovered a giant box of art supplies he'd forgotten about. He suddenly got an idea.

"Wiggles," said Blue Burt. "We can stop everything from changing. We can make it summer again."

"Then you can stay?" said Wiggles.

"If it's still summer, I can," said Blue Burt.

So the two of them got busy.

Wiggles gathered the fallen leaves. And Blue Burt flew them into the trees where he taped them back onto the branches. "There, now the leaves will stay in the trees," said Blue Burt. "Just like summer."

Next Blue Burt and Wiggles mixed the perfect shade of green paint, and then used it to color the grass green again. "That's how the grass should look," said Blue Burt. "Just like summer."

Wiggles drew bright flowers on construction paper. Blue Burt cut them out, and the two of them glued the flowers all around the woods.

"Flowers should always be in full bloom," said Blue Burt. "Just like summer."

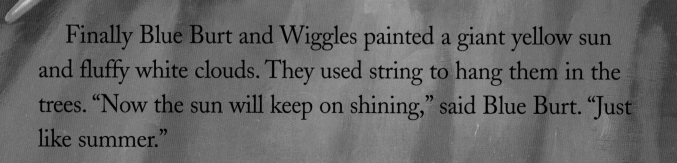

Finally Blue Burt and Wiggles painted a giant yellow sun and fluffy white clouds. They used string to hang them in the trees. "Now the sun will keep on shining," said Blue Burt. "Just like summer."

Blue Burt and Wiggles climbed down to admire their new summer . . . but when they got down to the ground, it wasn't summer at all.

The leaves had fallen again, the grass had been trampled, the paper flowers had disappeared, and even the string they'd used to hang the sun and clouds was gone.

"What happened?" said Blue Burt.

"Where did our summer go?" asked Wiggles.

So the two friends went off to find where their summer went.

They found the rabbits using their tape to make snowshoes for the coming winter. Summer was going away.

The bears were using their leftover paint to put a fresh coat on the cave walls before settling in for their naps. Summer was going away.

The squirrels were using their paper flowers to make warm quilts. Summer was going away.

The birds were using their string to tie up boxes and suitcases before heading south. Summer was gone.

Blue Burt and Wiggles couldn't fool the other animals.
And they couldn't fool the forest. Winter was coming.

Blue Burt didn't want to leave. But he couldn't wait any longer. So he packed his suitcase, said good-bye to his dear friend, Wiggles, and set out on his long flight south.

Blue Burt and Wiggles never once
forgot about each other. They wrote letters,
laughed on the phone, and they thought of each other often.

And even though they couldn't stop the woods from changing . . .

nothing could keep true friends apart forever.

For Mike Wigton (the real Wiggles)

SIMON & SCHUSTER BOOKS FOR YOUNG READERS
An imprint of Simon & Schuster Children's Publishing Division
1230 Avenue of the Americas, New York, New York 10020
Copyright © 2006 by Derek Anderson
All rights reserved, including the right of reproduction in whole or in part in any form.
SIMON & SCHUSTER BOOKS FOR YOUNG READERS is a trademark of Simon & Schuster, Inc.
Book design by Daniel Roode
The text for this book is set in ACaslon.
The illustrations for this book are rendered in acrylic paint.
Manufactured in China
2 4 6 8 10 9 7 5 3 1
Library of Congress Cataloging-in-Publication Data
Anderson, Derek, 1969-
Blue Burt and Wiggles / written and illustrated by Derek Anderson.— 1st ed.
p. cm.
Summary: When Blue Burt prepares to fly south with his other feathered companions,
he and his pal, Wiggles, wanting to prolong
their friendship, decide to trick Mother Nature into thinking that it is still summer.
ISBN-13: 978-1-4169-0593-6
ISBN-10: 1-4169-0593-6
[1. Birds—Fiction. II. Friendship—Fiction. III. Summer—Fiction.]
I. Title.
PZ7.A53313Bh 2006
[E]—dc22   2005029041